Published in Canada and the USA in 2020 by Groundwood Books

Groundwood Books / House of Anansi Press
groundwoodbooks.com

We gratefully acknowledge for their financial support of our publishing program the Canada Council for the Arts, the Ontario Arts Council and the Government of Canada.

Canada Council for the Arts | Conseil des Arts du Canada

ONTARIO ARTS COUNCIL
CONSEIL DES ARTS DE L'ONTARIO
an Ontario government agency
un organisme du gouvernement de l'Ontario

With the participation of the Government of Canada
Avec la participation du gouvernement du Canada | Canada

Library and Archives Canada Cataloguing in Publication
Title: I found hope in a cherry tree / Jean E. Pendziwol ; illustrated by Nathalie Dion.
Names: Pendziwol, Jean, author. | Dion, Nathalie, illustrator.
Identifiers: Canadiana (print) 20190218398 | Canadiana (ebook) 20190219149 | ISBN 9781773062204 (hardcover) | ISBN 9781773062211 (EPUB) | ISBN 9781773064239 (Kindle)
Classification: LCC PS8581.E55312 I2 2020 | DDC jC813/.6—dc23

The illustrations are a mix of traditional and digital paintings, cut, transformed and delicately placed in Photoshop.

Design by Michael Solomon
Printed and bound in China

For you, dear reader, for the times when
life feels unpredictable, confusing, scary …
remember to find hope.
— JEP

To the cat's father, Peter.
— ND

I Found Hope in a Cherry Tree

Jean E. Pendziwol Illustrated by Nathalie Dion

Groundwood Books House of Anansi Press Toronto Berkeley

I can see the sun in my shadow,
arms and legs
stretched in early morning
as large and long
as a giant's.

We play,
my shadow and I,
taking turns chasing,
first one
and then
the other.

Sometimes
my shadow
shrinks
to a small
mischievous
monkey,
and sometimes ...

it disappears.

I've learned it
never stays away
for long —

sometimes a few minutes,

sometimes a few hours,

sometimes a few days.

But it always comes back.

I can hear the wind tell stories,

whispering
to the trees,
making them
laugh
and
sigh.

The stories
dance, too,
chasing across the lake
until they climb ashore
to hush and hiss
in the sand.

When the stories
howl
like wolves
in winter
and creep
beneath the covers
to nibble my toes,
I remember that
the best way to tame
wolves is to tell
them a story.

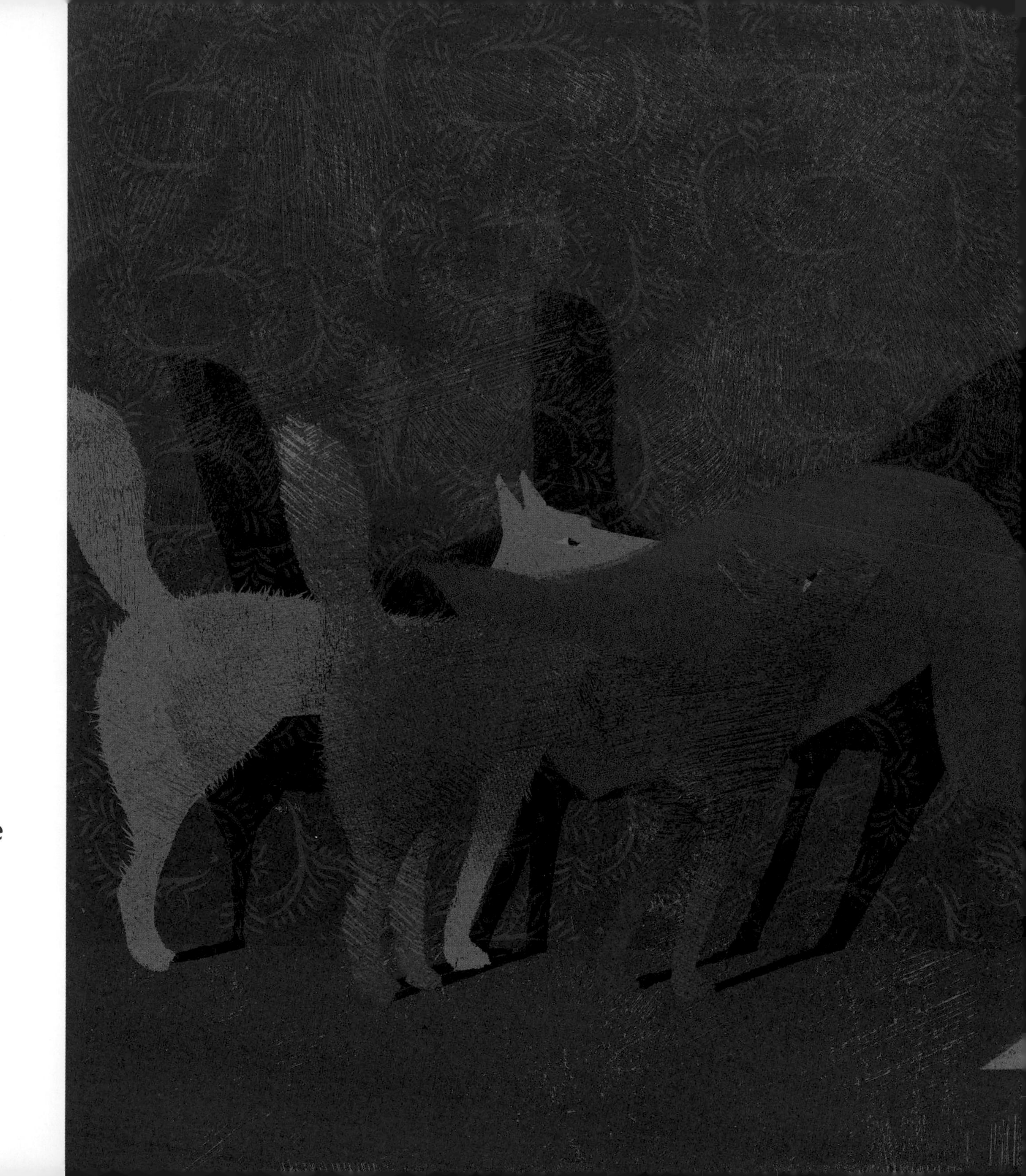

So I do.

I can taste clouds in snowflakes
that float gently,
fat and soft,
like a sweet dream
to melt on my tongue.

I collect them
on my mittens,
each one

perfect
and beautiful
and special.

Sometimes the snowflakes
toss and tumble
and arrive
icy and sharp
to prickle my cheeks
and freeze my nose.

But still
they taste
like clouds.

I found hope
in a cherry tree
that places tiny buds

on shivering,
leaf-bare branches in autumn,

knowing that
shadows
can disappear,
and stories
can howl like wolves,
and snowflakes
can be icy and sharp,
and there is no way
for the tree to be sure
that the buds will
ever bloom.

But the cherry tree
knows this:
it is hope
in autumn
that brings
flowers
in spring.